TITLE I

Vincennes Community School Corp.

Julian, Dream Doctor

By Ann Cameron

Illustrated by Ann Strugnell

A STEPPING STONE BOOK

Random House New York

To my cousin Charlotte, who, like Julian's mom, has a cool head and a warm heart

To Gerardo, who caught dozens of snakes when he was young, and thousands and thousands of frogs, and who is a rodeo champion and knows how to fix busted trucks

And to Maria, who has her whole life before her

Text copyright © 1990 by Ann Cameron. Illustrations copyright © 1990 by Ann Strugnell. All rights reserved under International and Pan-American Copyright Conventions. Published in the United States by Random House, Inc., New York, and simultaneously in Canada by Random House of Canada Limited, Toronto.

Library of Congress Cataloging-in-Publication Data:
Cameron, Ann, 1943– Julian, dream doctor / by Ann Cameron; illustrated by Ann Strugnell.
p.   cm.—(A Stepping stone book) Summary: Julian and Huey try to find the perfect birthday gift for Dad with amusing results.   ISBN 0-679-80524-9 (pbk.)—ISBN 0-679-90524-3 (lib. bdg.)   [1. Gifts—Fiction.   2. Birthdays—Fiction.   3. Family life—Fiction. 4. Afro-Americans—Fiction.]   I. Strugnell. Ann, ill.   II. Title.   PZ7.C1427Jr   1990 [Fic]—dc20   89-37562

Manufactured in the United States of America

25 24 23 22 21 20 19 18 17 16

Contents

1.

My Mom and My Dad

I love my mom and dad very much. This is what they are like.

My dad is a quick-moving man. He likes to play jokes, and he is full of surprises. Sometimes he even surprises himself.

My dad is a very good athlete. He is teaching me running, and basketball, and other sports.

When he runs, he is fast as fire. When he shoots baskets, he is quick as lightning. Afterward, when he rests, he is quiet as a turtle at the bottom of the sea.

The worst thing about my dad is how he gets impatient. My mom never does that.

When I want to talk to her, she will always listen. If I have a problem, she helps me work it out.

My mom is never in a hurry. If she meets somebody and asks, "How are you?" she always takes the time to hear the real answer.

My mom is like a cool green planet with forests and flowers and waterfalls. Any place around her is a good place to be.

Another thing about my mom: she never yells. She always talks softly.

Just to show you how she does not yell:

The day my little brother, Huey, fed his milk to the goldfish, my mom did not yell.

The day Huey practiced being a mechanic like Dad and put sugar in the gas tank of her car, my mom did not yell.

The day I tried to give Huey a bath from the upstairs window, but my mom was the person who walked under the window instead of Huey—she did not yell. She was NOT happy. But she did not yell.

This summer, when I found out about my dad's biggest dream and gave it to him for his birthday—even then, my mom did not yell.

My dad yelled, though. He yelled enough for two.

This is how it happened.

2.

My Very Good Idea

Every year we have a birthday party for my dad. Every year, the week before his birthday, my mom, Huey, and I go out and buy him a present.

This year was no different.

We went out. We got Dad a really good bowling ball. We wrapped it up and hid it in the back of the closet.

But then I started thinking. It would be nice to do something special for my dad. It would be nice to give him a surprise party and, besides the bowling ball, one special gift—something he had always dreamed of.

Once I thought of it, I could even imagine it happening. I could see myself showing Dad a mysterious box with a big bow on it, and Dad opening it and saying, "But Julian, nobody—nobody ever knew! This is what I've always dreamed of! Julian, you're a genius! This is the most unforgettable birthday that I have ever had!"

And then he would give me a big hug and be so excited he would lift me way off the ground.

I could imagine it so clearly that it seemed like it had already happened. I could see my mom being surprised too and saying, "Julian, how did you ever know what Dad wanted? You must have read his mind!"

The only thing I couldn't imagine was what was in the box. What did Dad dream of? What did he like more than anything? I didn't know.

I wanted to tell my best friend, Gloria, about my idea, but she was on vacation. So I told my little brother, Huey. I got Huey to practice asking Dad questions so we could find out his secret dream.

3.

Simple Things

It was night. My mom was at a meeting. My dad was supposed to have sent us to bed. But one nice thing about him is he usually forgets.

He and Huey and I were sitting on the front porch steps. Above the lawn, fireflies flashed their lights like tiny signaling flying saucers. In the little pine tree by the corner of the house we could hear the soft, thick sounds a bird makes, arranging its wings like blankets, getting ready to sleep.

It was a perfect time to get my dad to talk, a perfect time to find out what to get for his birthday.

"Dad," I said, "what do you love more than anything else in the world?"

My dad stretched his legs out. He smiled.

"You and Huey and Mom."

I was glad he said it. But it was no help in picking a special birthday present. We couldn't give Dad us. He already had us.

"But what do you like more than anything else in the world?" Huey asked. "Deep in your heart," he added.

My dad thought awhile.

"I like simple things. For instance—the ocean."

Huey's eyes widened. "That's awfully hard to wrap!" he said.

I kicked Huey's foot.

"What else do you like best of anything?" I asked.

"Something smaller," Huey suggested.

My dad smiled.

"Mountains," he said. "I like mountains, too."

I figured we could wrap a mountain, but I didn't see how we could carry it. Maybe we

could ask to have it delivered. The delivery-
men would have to be very, very big. I
imagined them coming to the door. "Pack-
age. Special birthday delivery for Ralph
Bates," they would say.

"Dad," Huey said, "deep in your heart,
what do you really like that's small?"

"Small?" Dad said. "An atom.

"Of course I've never seen one," he added.
"But I like the idea of it. I like to think how
tiny an atom is, and how much empty space
it has inside it, and how many parts it has,
all speeding around and knocking into one
another like a crazy ride at the fair."

"An atom!" I said. It would not be hard
to get. Forks, spoons, tables, dogs, hot dogs,
universes, and probably even monsters are all
made of atoms.

I am made of atoms too. I remembered
that and tried shaking one off my hand.

I thought it came loose. Then I tried to
pick it up off the step, but I couldn't tell if I
had picked it up or not. Maybe I squashed
it.

My dad was watching me.

"Skeeters biting you, Julian?" he asked.

"A little," I said. I wondered how many atoms there were in a mosquito. Probably about fifteen billion and one. We could give Dad a mosquito for his birthday and make a card that said: "Dear Dad, Here is the atom you asked for, plus fifteen billion extra." But no matter how much Dad liked atoms, I was pretty sure he didn't like skeeters that much.

"How about something—not quite so small?" Huey said.

My dad thought a long while.

Huey and I waited. I was sure we were finally going to find it out—Dad's real, catchable, wrappable, deliverable, secret dream.

Dad leaned back. He looked up.

"You know what I really like best of all?" he said.

"See way, way up there?

"That star."

4.

Brain Waves

My dad was at his shop. My mom was at her job. Huey was with me.

I was sitting in the backyard, working.

"Suppose Dad doesn't have one?" Huey asked.

"One what?" I said.

"A secret dream," Huey said.

"Dad is a grownup," I said. "Every grownup has a secret dream."

I thought I was right, but mostly I said it because I didn't want to give up my great idea.

"If Dad does have a secret dream, how are we going to find it out?" Huey asked.

"It's not going to be easy," I said. "We are going to have to work hard."

"With that stuff?" Huey said. He pointed all around me. I had every one of the big pots out in the yard, plus the eggbeater and the living room fan. I was tying them all together with wire. I had the fan and the eggbeater tied at the top.

"This is not stuff," I said. "This is equipment."

"What is it going to do?" Huey asked.

"Have you ever heard of brain waves?" I asked.

"No," Huey said.

"Just like there are waves in the ocean, there are invisible waves in the air. That's how radio and TV programs get to the house—on those waves."

"There aren't little people living in the TV set?" Huey said.

"No," I said, "there aren't." I wired the last pot into the equipment and tied the whole thing to the lowest branch of the big pine tree. I moved Huey so he was directly in front of it.

"Now," I said, "sit here with me."

Huey did.

"Brains also have waves," I said. "With this equipment, we will pick up signals from Dad's brain. If we concentrate on the signal, we will know what he really wants for his birthday."

"Okay," Huey said. He didn't sound con-
vinced.

"Close your eyes," I said. "It helps."

Huey did, and I closed my eyes too.

I concentrated on Dad. On what he
wanted, deep in his heart.

We sat a long time. I heard the pans moving in the wind. I heard the fan creak. I did not pick up any brain waves reflected from the equipment. After a while I heard something fall.

"Did you hear that?" Huey said.

"I did," I said.

"What was it?" Huey said.

"I think it was Mom's gumbo pot," I said. "Are you getting any messages from Dad?"

"No," Huey said. "But I think I got a message from Mom. About how she doesn't like the pots out on the lawn. Or the fan."

I opened my eyes. I looked at the brain wave receiver.

"Maybe you are right," I said. "Maybe we should take this stuff in."

We put the fan, the eggbeater, and the pots away. I was disappointed.

"It was such a great-looking machine! I can't figure out why it didn't work!" I said. "But never mind, I have another idea."

Huey and I got a rope out of the garage. We took it upstairs. We tied one end to the bedpost of our bed. The other end I tied tight around my waist.

I went to the window. The roof was very close and easy to get to, and it was practically flat. But I liked having the rope. It made me feel like a mountain climber. Also, I don't like taking chances.

I went out the window.

"Okay," I said. "Now Huey, you sit on the bed."

"Why?" Huey said.

"To weigh it down," I said.

"Why?" Huey said.

"In case I fall," I said. "You and the bed will hold me."

"Why would you fall?" Huey said. "The roof is practically flat."

"In case a giant wind comes," I said. "One that could blow me off the roof."

"But there's practically no wind," Huey said.

His questions were spoiling everything.

"Huey," I said, "just sit on the bed."

He did.

I looked around. I felt like an astronaut.

"One giant step forward," I said. "For science and for Dad."

I walked slowly like a moonwalker to where the TV antenna was attached to the roof. I held on to it with both hands.

"Safe!" I shouted. I shut my eyes and thought about Dad. About receiving his message. Using the TV antenna as a receiver, I might see a mental picture of his special present.

The picture would probably be in color, but I was also ready to receive in black and white.

A long time passed. Huey didn't say anything. Probably he had fallen asleep on the bed.

It was hot. My feet hurt. I got no signal.

Suddenly I heard a man's voice, low, soft, and urgent.

It was definitely a TV kind of voice. It sounded like Dad would sound if he was announcing a serious pain remedy.

"Julian," said the voice. "Julian."

It sounded like Dad's brain, waving!

"Receiving," I said softly, "receiving."

"Julian," said the voice, "my truck isn't working . . ."

"Truck broke?" I mentally transmitted. "Birthday present? New truck?"

"So I just jogged home for lunch. . . . Julian, this is your father speaking. . . ."

I wanted the voice to forget about jogging and get back on the subject.

"I know you're my father," I mentally transmitted. "Birthday present? New truck?"

The volume of the signal went up.

"Julian! Answer me! What are you DOING tied to your bed, on a rope out the window, talking to the TV antenna?"

I opened my eyes. I turned around. I let

go of the TV antenna. My brain waves shattered.

Dad was staring at me from the window. In color. In 3-D. Live.

"Dad!" I said. "Happy—" I was going to say happy birthday. But it wasn't his birthday, yet.

"Dad!" I said. "Happy day!"

5.

An Answer from the Deep

Gloria was at my front door. She was wearing a blue-green blouse with a design of foamy waves on it and a shell necklace. She sparkled like the sea.

"We had to come home from the beach early," she said, "because of my mother's business. But I'm glad, really. I missed you. And I had a feeling you were missing me."

"I missed you," I said. "I missed you a lot. And besides, we need you to help us. We have a problem." I told her about the surprise birthday party idea, and how we only had five days left and we still couldn't figure out what Dad wanted for a gift. And about

my mind-reading experiments that didn't work. And how hard it was to convince my dad that climbing out on the roof was a good thing to do if you wanted to be a TV repairman when you grew up.

"Personally," Gloria said, "I think you should be a scientist and not a TV repairman. I think you might invent something really great."

When my mom and dad got home, they invited Gloria to stay for lunch. We had turkey sandwiches, and my dad asked Gloria a lot about her vacation.

When we were done eating, he drank the last of his iced tea and yawned.

"Excuse me," he said. "Last night was a late bowling night. I sure could use a nap."

"Why don't you nap in the backyard in the hammock?" my mother suggested. "It's nice and cool out there."

"If you all don't mind—" he said.

The screen door closed behind him.

"You kids haven't been together for quite a while," my mom said, "so I'll do the dishes.

You can go outside and play. Just be careful not to wake Dad."

"All right," I said.

We went outside and talked. After a while we decided to go look at Dad to see if he was sleeping.

We crossed the grass on tiptoe. The hammock was in the shade, tied between two tall trees. Dad was hunched down inside it. His eyes were closed. He had a grass stem in his mouth. He was blowing air out gently through his nose.

"People look kind of funny when they sleep," Gloria said.

"Dad—Dad looks a little bit like a whale!" Huey whispered.

Dad muttered something in his sleep. We stepped back.

"I never knew Dad talked in his sleep," I said.

"There are people who are sleep talkers," Gloria said. "When they're sleeping, you can ask them questions and they will answer them. They always tell you the truth. Afterward, they don't remember that you asked them anything."

"Really?" I said. "We can try it on my dad. Maybe we will find out what he wants for his birthday!"

"He might wake up," Gloria said.

"He might wake up and be ANGRY," Huey said.

"It's our best chance!" I said. "We ought to try it. Huey, you go first!"

Huey didn't move.

"Forward!" I said. "Contact subject!"

Huey didn't move.

"We'll hold your hands," I said.

Gloria took one of Huey's hands and I took the other. We all walked closer to Dad. He wasn't muttering at all. He looked very peaceful.

Huey got ready. He held our hands tighter.

"Wha-d'you-wan-f'yer-birthday?" All his words squirted out at once, like ink from an octopus.

Dad didn't answer. He made a little groan

and waved a hand in front of his face, like a whale flipper.

We didn't even whisper. We waited two minutes.

"Try again, Huey," I said softly.

Huey said, "No."

"I'll try," Gloria whispered.

"Mr. Bates," Gloria murmured, "what do you want for your birthday?"

Dad opened his lips. His grass stem fell on his shirt. His lips closed again.

"Maybe he's not a real sleep talker," she whispered. "Not everybody is."

"Anyhow, I'll try," I said.

I moved up to the hammock. I was afraid Dad was too much asleep. I picked up the grass stem he had dropped. Very lightly, I brushed it against his arm.

I tried to make my voice serious—like mine, but coming from Mars.

"Are? You? Dreaming?" I asked.

Dad moved a little. The hammock rocked. We jumped back.

Dad's lips opened. "Yes," he said.

"Do? You? Know? Your? Birthday? Is? Coming?" I asked.

Dad's foot twitched.

"Yes," he said.

"What? Do? You? Want? For? Your? Birthday?" I asked.

Dad didn't answer.

"For. Your. Birthday," I repeated.

Dad didn't answer.

I hoped he was thinking it over.

"Your dream," I suggested. "Your. Biggest. DREAM."

Dad made another tiny groan. His whale body swayed the hammock. He looked as if he were speaking underwater.

"Two snakes," he said. "Big ones."

Could it really be true?

"For your birthday," I said. "What do you want more than anything?"

"Two snakes," Dad said again. "Big ones."

6.

Blue Fang's Children

"Do you actually like snakes?" Gloria asked.

"I don't know," I said. "Of course, they don't scare me. But they kind of make me nervous."

Gloria, Huey, and I were walking in the park by the river.

We had on long pants and our strongest, toughest shoes. I had Dad's hatchet and a piece of string. Huey carried an old pillowcase. Gloria had her jackknife and a book from the library, *All About Snakes*. We each had a long, curved stick for snake catching. We had practiced using the sticks for two days.

"Would you look at the map in the book again, Gloria?" I said. "The one that shows there are no poisonous snakes where we live?"

Gloria bent her head over the map. "It still says the same. Should I read you some more about snakes?"

"All right," I said.

" 'Snakes have very poor eyesight. They do not taste with their tongues. Instead, they use their tongues to smell and to sense the vibrations of other animals' movements.

" 'Snakes are shy. Snakes are friends of humankind. Snakes eat species that are our enemies, such as mosquitoes and rats.

" 'There is almost no reason for people to be afraid of snakes. Pythons in India may have eaten small babies—' "

"BABIES!" Huey said. He grabbed the handle of my hatchet.

" '. . . but,' " Gloria continued, " 'this has never been proved. It is more likely that the babies were eaten by leopards.' "

"LEOPARDS!" Huey said. "I want to go home!"

I held Huey's arm. "Huey," I said, "we aren't in India! That's another country! And there aren't any leopards in the park. Probably there aren't even any snakes, either. We're just making a try."

"I want to go home," Huey said.

"Just one little try," I said. "One little

try to make Dad really happy on his birthday."

Huey was silent. Wild animals moved in
the high tree branches. Huey looked up. "All
right," he said. "But I won't stay unless I
can carry the hatchet."

I gave it to him. We started on down the
trail. My right hand felt light and empty
without the hatchet. I poked at the grass at
the side of the trail with my snake-catching
stick.

"Should I read some more?" Gloria asked.

"Okay," I said.

" 'Very few snakes are poisonous. Snakes
do not bite people unless they are cornered
and have no way of escape. Of course, if you
are trying to collect a snake to study at home,
it will try to bite. So be careful!'

"More?" Gloria said. She turned a page.

" 'To suck the blood out of a poisonous
snake bite, first cut the bitten place with a
jackknife. Then—' "

"BLOOD! Ugh! Don't read that part!" I
said.

Gloria closed the book. We all looked around.

We were farther into the park than we had ever gone before. Sometimes the tall grass swayed higher than our heads. In some places big boulders looked like a giant's bowling game. As if he had been throwing them for fun, to knock trees down. Below the boulders gray, twisted tree stumps looked like broken arms climbing out of the river.

"Well," Gloria said, "at least it's a nice, bright, sunny—"

Something hissed.

We looked down. A snake was at our feet. It was thick and long. It was yellow, with bright red spots outlined in black. It moved like a bullet. It moved like an express train. In a second it had zoomed away.

"It had blue teeth!" Huey said.

"It did not have blue teeth!" Gloria said. "No snake has blue teeth. It went into its burrow, that's all. And it's a giant! Just the kind your dad wants for his birthday!"

Sometimes I wish Gloria was not so brave.

I looked at my snake-catching stick. It looked strong enough to stop a marshmallow at a marshmallow roast. If the marshmallow didn't put up a fight.

"This snake-catching stick," I said. "It doesn't look strong enough to stop that snake. . . ."

"The-the-the hatchet couldn't stop that snake!" Huey said.

"My dad doesn't want chopped snake anyhow," I said. "He wants live snakes."

"He-he-he wants n-n-nice fr-fr-friendly snakes," Huey said. "He-he-he doesn't want—"

The grass rustled behind us. We jumped. We turned.

There were two snakes in the grass, spotted like Blue Fang, but smaller.

Probably with their bad eyesight they couldn't see us. Probably they were waiting for the vibrations when we moved.

Silently, we crouched. Without a sound, just the way we had practiced, we lifted our snake-catching sticks. Faster than old Blue

Fang had moved, Gloria and I brought our curved sticks down. Right behind the head, our sticks pinned the snakes to the ground.

"We've got them!" Gloria said.

The snakes raised their heads angrily and swayed them from side to side. Because of the sticks, they could only move their heads about an inch. Their red smeller-tongues flickered desperately. Their long, strong bodies writhed and coiled. It was scary to see them coil. But the back parts of their bodies couldn't hurt us. And no matter how much they moved, they couldn't escape. Our sticks held them tight to the ground.

"We—we did it!" Huey said.

"Right!" I said. "Now, hold the pillow-case open! Just leave a little narrow space at the top!"

Huey did. Quickly I reached down. With my thumb and my first finger I grabbed my snake between the stick and the front of its head. I let go of the stick and lifted the snake up. Then I took hold of its tail with my other hand and held the snake upside down. I guided its head into the opening in the pillowcase and let it slide down. It didn't fight.

It didn't even act angry anymore. It just tumbled down into the bottom of the pillowcase and stayed there.

"Now Gloria's," I said.

Gloria grabbed her snake just the way I had grabbed mine. Soon hers was in the pillowcase too.

Huey held up the bag and looked at the outlines of the snakes' bodies through the cloth.

"Dad wants two big snakes," Huey said. "But are you sure he wants them *this* big?"

"I'm sure," I said.

I took the heavy bag from Huey and tied it shut with string. Then I lifted it and held it high.

"To the greatest birthday present ever!" I said.

"We really did it!" said Gloria.

"Of course!" I said.

But deep in my heart I was amazed, amazed, amazed. The way you are when you imagine doing something you are pretty sure you really can't do, and then—unbelievable!—you succeed.

7.

The Prisoners and the Party

When we got home, we moved the snakes into a new house—a big cardboard box with air holes in it. We hid the box in our room. (Actually, our room is so messy that as soon as you put anything in it, that thing is hidden.)

Every few minutes we would open the box a crack and look in. The snakes stayed completely still. Even though they must have sensed us, they did not move. Sometimes we reached in and touched them. They still did not move. Their skins were dry and smooth—black as ink, yellow as the sun, and red as red, red leaves in autumn. We called the longer one Son of Blue Fang and the shorter one Daughter of Blue Fang, but it was hard to tell them apart. They were both almost four feet long.

We didn't take our rabbits, Jake and Beansprout, to meet them. We didn't think the rabbits were ready for the shock.

But in the night, I got a shock myself. I woke up hearing a very strange sound. The snakes were moving, rubbing their big bodies against the sides of the box, looking for a way out.

I figured that by nature they were night hunters. Just like prisoners making a jailbreak, they knew that they couldn't get away safely in the day, when the sounds of people were all around them. They had waited until the house was quiet, until it was dark. Then they tested the box.

I was sure it was strong. But still I got up and put a few more pieces of tape on the lid, just in case.

Gloria's book said that the snakes only

ate once a week, so we didn't give them food. But we did put a saucer of water in the box.

A second night passed; the morning of Dad's birthday came. Mom knocked on our door. We shoved the box under the bed.

"I'll be back just before five," Mom said, "and Dad will be back just after. We can have the party then and give him his present. And it would be nice if you invited Gloria."

"She already knows," I said. "She wouldn't want to miss it."

Just after Mom left, Gloria came over.

When we finished checking on Dad's snakes, we got out peanuts for the party and made lemonade. Then we decorated the house. We mixed food coloring and powdered sugar and drew a snake on Dad's birthday cake with toothpicks. Then we drew snakes on some paper napkins, and we made a snake out of wire and crepe paper that we fastened to the kitchen cabinets and to the light on the living room ceiling. The big snake took two hours to make. It had a red, fringy tongue, and it stretched through two rooms. It was even bigger than old Blue Fang.

Then we put a bow on the snakes' cardboard box and a little wrapping paper. They moved a lot. It was probably the first time they were ever wrapped. We were careful not to cover their breathing holes.

At 4:45 everything was ready. We carried the snakes' box into the living room and hid it behind a chair. We set the cake and the napkins on the kitchen table.

Then we stood and looked around.

We were really proud. Our party was going to be perfect—the best party a dad could ever have. Especially if he secretly loved snakes, the way Dad did.

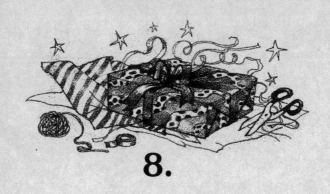

8.

Dream Delivery

"Julian! Huey! What are these decorations?"

It was Mom's voice. She was not yelling, but she did sound perturbed.

Huey and Gloria and I went into the kitchen.

"We got a special present for Dad," I said. "Also, we made special decorations."

"Snake decorations?" Mom said. "And what is the present?"

"We'd like to keep it a surprise," I said. "If you don't mind."

"But why snake decorations?" Mom said.

"Dad loves snakes," I said.

My mother looked very surprised. "I never knew that! I never knew Dad even thought about snakes. How do you know Dad loves snakes?"

"He told us," I said. I thought of telling Mom we had interrogated Dad while he was sleeping. I decided she might not approve of that. I decided not to tell her.

"Told you?" Mom said.

"Yes," I said, "we asked him right straight out what he wanted more than anything, and he said, 'Two big snakes.' "

My mom looked as if she didn't believe me.

"You're sure you really heard Dad right? You're sure he didn't say 'Two thick shakes'? You know how Dad loves milk shakes."

"It wasn't shakes," Huey said. "It was snakes."

"I was there," Gloria said. "He really said it. 'Two big snakes.' "

Mom glanced at the clock. It was almost five.

"It's hard to believe," she said. "But if you all asked him, I suppose it must be true.

"I hear Dad," she said. "Quick! Let's put the candles in the cake!"

We did. We stuck in all thirty-five of them. And then Dad walked in the door.

"Happy birthday!" we said, all together.

"Thank you!" Dad said. He got a big smile on his face and gave us all hugs. Then he felt the fringy tongue of our crepe paper snake in his hair and looked up.

"My," he said, "what an interesting birthday decoration. A very well made— snake." He moved so he wasn't standing under it.

"We knew you'd like it!" I said.

"Have some lemonade," Mom said.

"Thanks!" Dad said.

She poured us all lemonade.

My dad put a napkin around his glass.

"A toast to my wonderful family," he said, "and to Gloria, a wonderful girl."

He smiled and raised his glass, and so did we.

My dad looked harder at his napkin, and then at ours.

He raised his eyebrows. "Snakes again!"

he said. "My, what an interesting—party theme."

He looked at the napkin again.

"Blue fangs on this one!" he said. "How—special." He gulped all his lemonade at once and choked on it a little.

"Excuse me," he said.

He set his glass on the table. The tongue of the crepe paper snake caught his hair.

Dad shook his head to get loose.

"It's so nice to come home to a surprise party! And such a surprising surprise party!"

He looked up at the crepe paper snake again.

"How far does this thing go?" he asked.

"Look and see!" Huey said.

We all followed it through the living room to its other end.

"What an unusual birthday!" Dad said.

"Would you like your first present?" Mom said. She went to the closet and got the box with the bowling ball.

Dad opened it.

"Wonderful!" Dad said. He lifted it and felt its weight. He moved as if he were going to throw it. "I'm sure this will improve my game," he said.

"Happy birthday, Mr. Bates," Gloria said. She handed Dad a tiny box.

He opened it. It had a seashell inside.

"I found it on my vacation," Gloria said. "I thought you'd like it."

"It's beautiful," Dad said. "I'll keep it on my desk at the shop."

"There's one last present," I said.

Gently, we carried the big cardboard box out from behind the chair.

"Here it is!" Huey said. "From me, and from Julian, and from Gloria."

"Hmm," said my dad. "Hmm, what a nice red ribbon! What a big box."

He lifted the cover.

"It's your dream," I said.

Dad looked at me.

Dad's arm jerked. The cover of the box flew up in the air and hit the living room ceiling. Son of Blue Fang raised his head and slithered out of the box. He started crawling for an open kitchen cabinet.

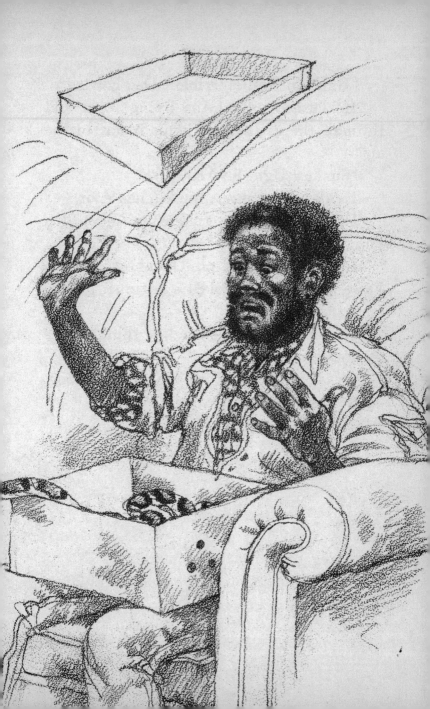

"Ugh! Snakes! Horrible!" Dad howled.

He rushed out of the living room and through the kitchen with his hands in the air.

"Snakes! Ugh! SNAKES!!!"

He disappeared out the kitchen door.

I closed the kitchen cabinet on Son of Blue Fang.

I closed the box on Daughter of Blue Fang. She (or he) looked a little surprised, for a snake.

"Julian," my mother said, "I think there's been a very big mistake."

We all moved toward the kitchen door, where Dad had disappeared.

9.

The End of a Dream

Dad was in the front yard, standing braced against a tree.

He looked up at us, but he didn't smile at all. He looked as if he didn't want to talk. He was sweating, even though it wasn't very hot. He took out his handkerchief and mopped his forehead. Then he looked at us and frowned.

"My thirty-fifth birthday! It's a good-sized birthday—an important birthday. And what do I get?"

"Snakes!" shouted Huey.

Dad shook his head. "I suppose it must

mean something. But I don't know what."
He kept on looking at us.

We didn't know what to say.

He put his handkerchief away and
hunched up as if he were cold.

"I don't understand it. HOW did I get
SNAKES for my birthday!"

"Ralph," my mother said soothingly, "the
children say you told them it's what you
wanted."

"I told them?" My dad wiped his brow
again.

"In the hammock," I said. "Last Saturday. You were sleeping. We sneaked up—
Gloria and Huey and me. We asked you what
you wanted for your birthday. I asked you
your biggest dream.

"You answered in your sleep. You said,
'Two snakes. Big ones.'

"And I asked you again what you wanted
for your birthday, and you repeated it, word
for word."

"Mr. Bates, I'm sorry," Gloria said. "We
thought—I thought—people always tell the
truth when they're asleep."

My father sighed an enormous sigh. He put his head in his hands and closed his eyes.

"Saturday," he said. "The hammock. Now I remember. I was dreaming. My biggest dream. My biggest, most horrible dream. The one where snakes wriggle around and around and turn into living neckties. . . . And then, just before the part where they turn into neckties, I heard Julian's voice. It was like a rescue.

" 'Dream,' Julian said. He said, 'dream,' as if he were in my dream telling me it wasn't real. The snakes . . . weren't real. A little while after that, I woke up.

"I have had this bad dream practically all my life," he said, "but I never told anybody before."

He sat down at the foot of the tree. We went and sat with him.

"I've been scared of snakes all my life," Dad said. "I don't really know why."

"I was scared of them too," I said. "But then, when we went and caught those two in the woods, it got better. I got used to them. I'm not scared anymore."

"That's good," my dad said. He tried to smile. "I'm proud of you for getting over being scared."

He sat very quietly for a moment. "If I could," he said, "I would like to get over it. Get over being afraid of snakes."

"The best way," my mom said, "is to look at them. And have them around for a few

days. Then put them back in the woods. They are probably suffering. They are probably very scared too."

Dad cleared his throat. "Julian, Huey, Gloria," he said, "I do appreciate the work you did to get me what you thought I wanted. It just takes some getting used to."

He sighed. "Would you please bring them

out? I *will* look at them. Maybe I can learn to see them the way you do."

I went inside. Son (or Daughter) of Blue Fang was curled in the corner of the kitchen cabinet. I used a glove potholder and gently picked him (or her) up behind the head. I put him (or her) in the box with his sister (or brother) and took the box outside to Dad.

I set it down in front of him.

Dad stared at the box. He took a deep breath, like he was about to jump into deep water.

Carefully he opened the box. He peered down into it.

Huey and Gloria and I held our breath.

"The patterns in their skin are very beautiful," he said.

He stared at the snakes some more, and then he did an amazing thing. Slowly he lowered his hand into the box until it actually touched Son of Blue Fang on the back. Son of Blue Fang didn't move. Maybe he liked the warmth of Dad's hand. Maybe he was tired of being scared and fighting and running away.

"Maybe it feels like I do," Dad said. He pulled his hand back and gently closed the box.

"Where did you get the snakes?" he asked.

"We found them in the park," Huey said.

"We could take them back right now. Right today," I said.

"No," Dad said, "I want to do what Mom said. I want to keep them for a little while.

"If I can get used to them, Julian really will have rescued me. He'll be my dream doctor. He'll have helped to cure me of my one and only bad dream."

My dad stood up. My mom did too.

"Would you like your cake now?" she said. "We could have it outside on the lawn."

"I'd like that," Dad said.

Huey and Gloria and I went inside. We lit every candle on my dad's cake, and then we carried it out. Mom sang "Happy Birthday" with us, and Dad smiled.

Then he looked at all the candles burning on his thirty-fifth-birthday cake and smiled a littler smile. For a second I could imagine the way Dad must have looked when he was just a kid like me.

"All my life I've been—well, probably not the bravest, bravest person, but—brave enough," said my dad.

He shrugged. "And here I am, thirty-five years old . . . still learning not to be scared of things."

He mopped his face again with his hand- kerchief. Then he shut his eyes and made his birthday wish.

He opened his eyes. He held my hand and Huey's.

He took a gigantic breath and blew out all the candles at once.